For all the people who made the UK
feel like home for me, and for the new friends
I've made in Los Angeles.

Text and illustrations © 2018 by Nicola O'Byrne

Published by arrangement with Walker Books Ltd., 87 Vauxhall Walk, London SE11 5HJ

First published 2018 by Walker Books Ltd.

This edition published 2019 in the United States of America by Flyaway Books,
100 Witherspoon Street, Louisville, Kentucky 40202-1396. Online at www.flyawaybooks.com.

19 20 21 22 23 24 25 26 27 28–10 9 8 7 6 5 4 3 2 1

Book design by Allison Taylor
Text set in Intro

Library of Congress Cataloging-in-Publication Data
Names: O'Byrne, Nicola, author, illustrator.
Title: Where is home, Daddy Bear? / Nicola O'Byrne.
Description: Louisville, Kentucky : Flyaway Books, 2019. | "First published
   2018 by Walker Books Ltd." | Summary: During a long journey from their
   old house to the new, Evie Bear asks her father many questions as he
   reassures her that home is much more than a place.
Identifiers: LCCN 2019001545 | ISBN 9781947888142 (alk. paper)
Subjects: | CYAC: Moving, Household--Fiction. | Fathers and
   daughters--Fiction. | Home--Fiction. | Bears--Fiction.
Classification: LCC PZ7.O1637 Whe 2019 | DDC [E]--dc23
LC record available at https://lccn.loc.gov/2019001545

PRINTED IN CHINA

Most Flyaway Books are available at special quantity discounts when purchased in bulk by corporations,
organizations, and special-interest groups. For more information, please e-mail SpecialSales@flyawaybooks.com.

Where Is Home, Daddy Bear?

Nicola O'Byrne

Evie Bear was hiding.
She didn't want to go.

"I'll miss it too," said Dad.

"We've made so many memories here."

"Why do we have to move?" asked Evie Bear.

"Well," said Dad, "everything changes eventually. And in the beginning, change can feel sad. But it doesn't always. If nothing changed, there would be no more birthday parties."

Dad helped Evie pack her books in the very last box and locked the front door for the very last time. Evie felt . . . heavy.

"Goodbye, home," said Dad.

"Goodbye, home," said Evie.

"Dad," asked Evie Bear, as Dad squeezed the last box in the truck, "how will I make new friends?"

"Hmm," said Dad. "Why don't you start with a smile? Those are the same everywhere."

As they set off, Dad said, "I spy with my little eye something beginning with *L*."

"Leaf?" guessed Evie.

She already knew that leaves were Dad's favorite thing
to spy. Evie guessed "traffic light," "car," and "pigeons"
as the city began to fade away.

"Dad," asked Evie Bear, "what if I don't like the new home?"

Dad thought about this. "At first, everything might seem different. But after a while, you will notice all the things that are the same. And soon enough, you will find new things that you like."

Evie didn't reply. For a very long time, she looked out the window. And then, in a small voice, she said, "This is the farthest from home I have ever been."

Evie Bear's tummy let out a long rumble, and Dad had a very good idea: blueberry pancakes, just like the ones they made at home.

"Where am I from now?" asked Evie Bear as they ate.

"Our old home, or our new one?"

"Maybe a little bit of both," Dad answered. "We are all a mixture of the places we've been, the place we are now, and the places we're going to go."

Back on the road, Dad and Evie Bear drove for a long time.
Dad turned on the radio, and they sang together loudly
as the sun began to set.

"We're almost at the campsite," announced Dad.
"We'll stop here tonight
and keep going
in the morning."

Dad tucked Evie Bear in,
but she couldn't sleep.
"Dad," said Evie,
"I'm not sure where
home is anymore."

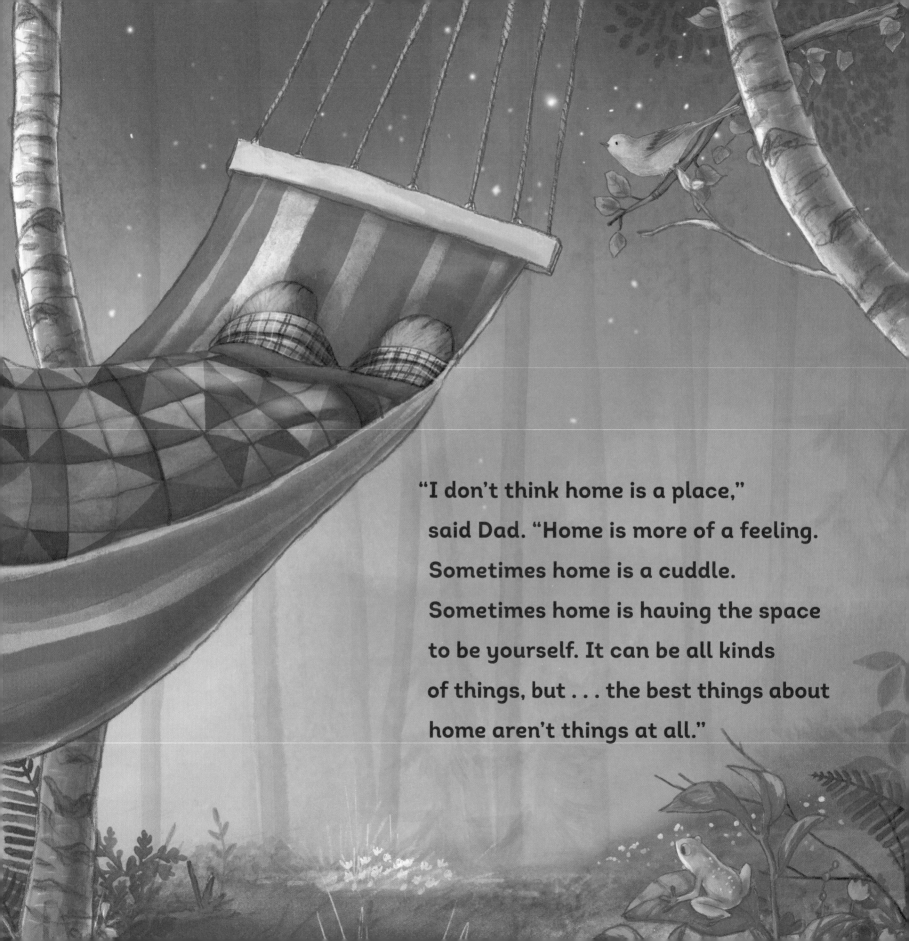

"I don't think home is a place,"
said Dad. "Home is more of a feeling.
Sometimes home is a cuddle.
Sometimes home is having the space
to be yourself. It can be all kinds
of things, but . . . the best things about
home aren't things at all."

The next morning Evie Bear and Dad were up early.
Today they would reach their new home.

Tree after tree passed by before Evie asked,
"Dad, are we there yet?"
Dad didn't reply.

"Dad," asked Evie, "are we lost?"

Dad scrunched up his big, furry brow.

"I know we're close," he said.

"We just need to find the river . . ."

"I have an idea," said Evie. "I spy with my little eye something beginning with *B*."

"Maybe a . . . bird?" guessed Dad.

"I spy with my little eye something beginning with *T*," said Evie.

"A . . . tree?" guessed Dad.

"I spy with my little eye something beginning with . . . *R*!" said Evie.

CB4 2JD

"RIVER! THE RIVER!" shouted Dad.
"There it is, Evie! You found it!"

"Dad," asked Evie, "were you scared
when we were lost?"

"A little," said Dad, "but I wasn't
really lost with you beside me."

Dad unlocked the front door
to their new home. Evie Bear
felt flitter-fluttery butterflies
in her tummy.

She felt . . . excited!

"I think I know where home is," said Evie Bear,

as she helped Dad unpack her blanket and books.

"Home is people who love you. Home is me and you."

Then Dad read Evie Bear three bedtime stories, and,
cuddled up in bed, surrounded by home . . .
they both fell fast asleep.